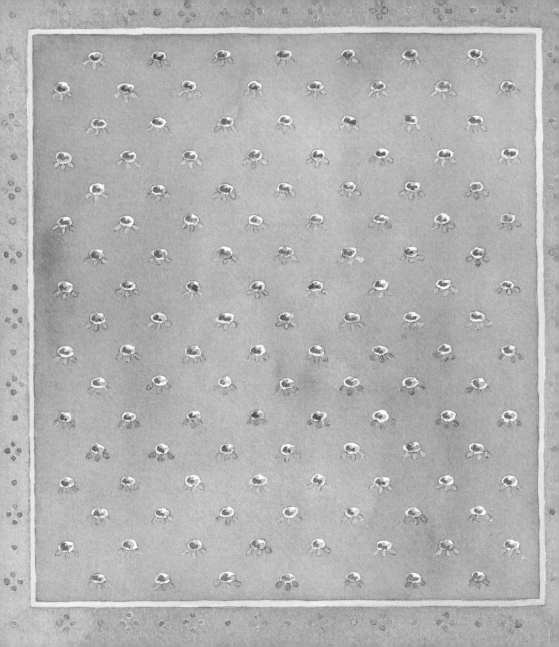

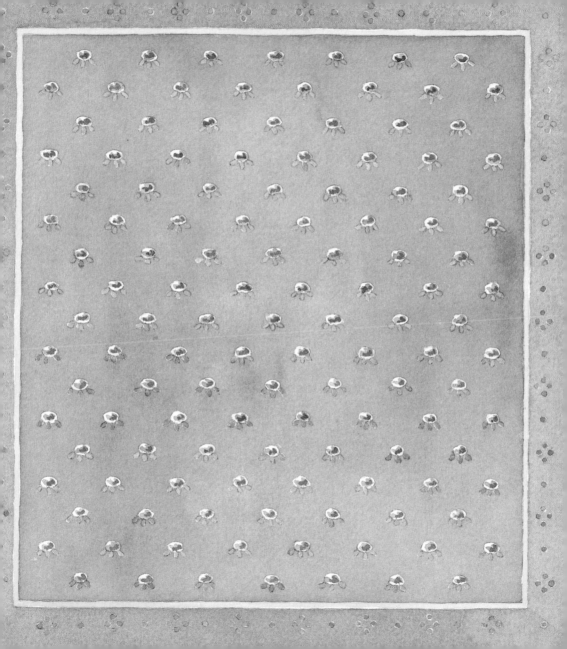

For Jean-Paul,
for the "land where the Bong-tree grows,"
and for Michelle for everything.
D.K.

First published 1996 by Walker Books Ltd
87 Vauxhall Walk, London SE11 5HJ
This edition published 2009
2 4 6 8 10 9 7 5 3 1
Illustrations © 1996 Dana Kubick
The right of Dana Kubick to be identified as illustrator of this work has been asserted by her in
accordance with the Copyright, Designs and Patents Act 1988
This book has been typeset in Garamond Educational
Printed in China
British Library Cataloguing in Publication Data:
a catalogue record for this book is available from the British Library.
ISBN 978-0-7445-3950-9
www.walker.co.uk

The Owl and the Pussy-Cat

Edward Lear
Illustrated by Dana Kubick

WALKER BOOKS

AND SUBSIDIARIES

LONDON · BOSTON · SYDNEY · AUCKLAND

The Owl and the Pussy-cat
   went to sea
In a beautiful pea-green boat,
They took some honey,
   and plenty of money,
Wrapped up in a five-pound note.

The Owl looked up
   to the stars above,
And sang to a small guitar,
   "O lovely Pussy!
   O Pussy, my love,
What a beautiful Pussy you are,
   You are,
   You are!
What a beautiful Pussy you are!"

Pussy said to the Owl,
   "You elegant fowl!
How charmingly sweet you sing!
O let us be married!
    too long we have tarried:
But what shall we do for a ring?"

They sailed away,
    for a year and a day,
To the land where
    the Bong-tree grows

And there in a wood
   a Piggy-wig stood
With a ring at the end of his nose,
   His nose,
   His nose,
With a ring at the end of his nose.

"Dear Pig, are you willing
    to sell for one shilling
Your ring?"
    Said the Piggy, "I will."
So they took it away,
    and were married next day
By the Turkey who lives on the hill.

They dined on mince,
    and slices of quince,
Which they ate
    with a runcible spoon;

And hand in hand,
  on the edge of the sand,
They danced by the light of the moon,
  The moon,
  The moon,
They danced by the light of the moon.

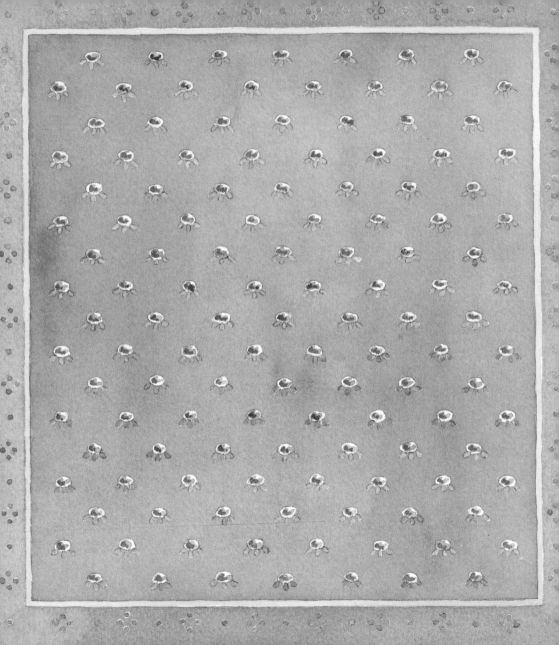

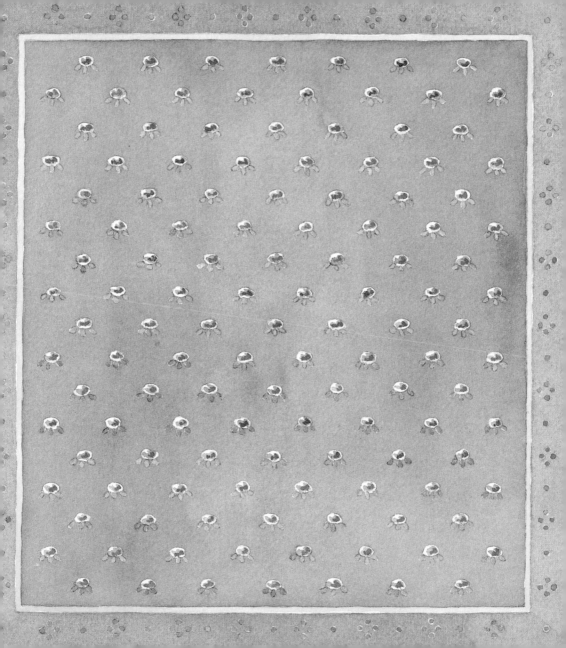